D0564548

The Amazing Panda Adventure

Adapted by Francine Hughes
From the
Screenplay by Jeff Rothberg and Laurice Elehwany
Story by John Wilcox & Steven Alldredge

SCHOLASTIC INC.
New York Toronto London Auckland Sydney

THE
AMAZING
PANDA
ADVENTURE

WARNER BROS. PRESENTS
A LEE RICH/GARY FOSTER PRODUCTION A CHRISTOPHER CAIN FILM "THE AMAZING PANDA ADVENTURE"
STEPHEN LANG YI DING RYAN SLATER MUSIC BY WILLIAM ROSS EXECUTIVE PRODUCER GABRIELLA MARTINELLI
STORY BY JOHN WILCOX & STEVEN ALLDREDGE SCREENPLAY BY JEFF ROTHBERG AND LAURICE ELEHWANY
PRODUCED BY LEE RICH, JOHN WILCOX, GARY FOSTER AND DYLAN SELLERS
DIRECTED BY CHRISTOPHER CAIN

PG PARENTAL GUIDANCE SUGGESTED
SOME MATERIAL MAY NOT BE SUITABLE FOR CHILDREN

WARNER BROS. FAMILY ENTERTAINMENT
A TIME WARNER ENTERTAINMENT COMPANY

No part of this publication may be reproduced in whole or in part, or stored in a retrieval system, or transmitted in any form or by any means, electronic, mechanical, photocopying, recording, or otherwise, without written permission of the publisher. For information regarding permission, write to Scholastic Inc., 555 Broadway, New York, NY 10012.

ISBN 0-590-55207-4

Copyright © 1995 by Warner Bros.
All rights reserved. Published by Scholastic Inc.

12 11 10 9 8 7 6 5 4 3 2 1
5 6 7 8 9/9 0/0

Printed in the U.S.A.   24

First Scholastic printing, August 1995

Ryan Tyler stood at the airport gate, on his way to China to visit his father. Twelve-year-old Ryan hadn't seen his father for two years, and he was feeling nervous.

"My dad does important work," Ryan told himself as he hugged his mom good-bye. "He's trying to save the giant panda from extinction. That's why I haven't seen him for so long. That's why he hasn't answered my letters."

Ha! Ryan thought. I bet Dad just doesn't care. And here I am, leaving my best friend, Johnny, and my favorite TV show behind!

Still, Ryan boarded the plane, and seventeen hours later landed at Cheng Du Airport. Inside the terminal, Ryan stretched his legs and looked anxiously for his father. People bustled all around speaking rapid Chinese. But Ryan didn't see his father anywhere. Feeling lost and alone, Ryan followed a group of government officials outside. The men got onboard a bus with a picture of a panda on its side.

Ryan had seen the picture before—in a pamphlet from the panda reserve where his father worked. So Ryan got on, too. And a minute later he jounced along, watching bamboo trees and bright flowers whiz past his window.

At the panda reserve, Ryan's dad stood by a rickety old tractor, ordering workers to load equipment onto its trailer. "Hurry!" Michael Tyler cried. "A mother panda and her baby are in danger!"

Everyone scurried about. They knew if anything happened to the panda cub, officials would close the reserve down. There'd be no reason to keep it open; the panda would soon be extinct.

"Come on!" Michael shouted to his assistants—an old man named Chu and his young granddaughter, Ling. "The mother panda is wearing a tracking collar. It will lead us right to her!"

Just then the airport bus rattled up the road. Ryan smiled as Michael rushed right over. "You're early," said Michael. Ryan opened his mouth to answer. But then he realized his dad was talking to the government officials.

"Yes, Dr. Tyler," said one official. "We are here to make a report on the progress of the reserve."

"But we aren't ready!" Michael's voice trailed off when he noticed Ryan. "Ryan?" he said, surprised. "What are you doing here? Your plane's not due until eleven tonight."

"Eleven this *morning*," said Ryan, thinking his dad would have known that —if he cared.

Michael felt bad. He knew what Ryan was thinking. But he had to find that panda! "You must be tired," he told Ryan, leading him through the compound. "I'll take you to your quarters. Then I've got to go into the forest."

Ryan watched his father head for the tractor where Chu and Ling waited. "I didn't come all this way to take a nap!" he shouted.

"It's too dangerous," his father said. "I promise I'll be back soon."

"That's what you said two years ago," Ryan said stubbornly.

A few minutes later the tractor left the compound, with Ryan sitting up front with his dad.

"The American children are spoiled!" Ling sputtered to her grandfather, angry that they were stuck in the back.

Ryan held on tight as they rode over bumpy trails high up in the hills.

At last the tracking equipment beeped, and Michael slowed to a stop. "The pandas are close by," he whispered.

Suddenly they heard the sound of heavy footsteps. "Poachers!" cried Ling. "They want to steal the baby panda and sell him!"

Michael jumped off the tractor and quickly made his way to a small clearing. Two poachers were closing in on a panda and her cub! Without stopping to think, Michael raced over. The men turned, surprised. Then, quick as lightning, they struck out. *Thud!* Michael fell heavily to the ground, twisting his leg. Grabbing the little cub, the poachers rushed away.

"What was that?" cried Ryan when he heard the noise. But Chu and Ling didn't answer. They were already racing to find out.

Moving more slowly, Ryan edged over to the clearing. At the sight of his father hurt and in pain, Ryan caught his breath. Chu tended to Michael's leg. Ling radioed for a helicopter. And Ryan just stood by helplessly. He wanted to put his arms around his dad. He wanted to comfort him. But something held him back—the thought that his father didn't want him around.

"We have to protect the mother panda," Michael gasped. "The baby needs her milk. Without it the cub is lost...and so is the reserve."

Moments later the helicopter arrived, and the pilot moved the mother panda inside. Ling took off the panda's tracking collar, so the animal could breathe easier, then stuck it in her backpack. Ryan craned his neck to look inside the copter. There was one seat left.

"Ryan, you get up front," Michael told him. "I'll take the next one with Ling and Chu."

But Michael was hurt, and Ryan knew he needed help. "I can wait here," he said, trying to sound brave.

Michael shook his head, uncertain. But finally, wincing with pain, he climbed aboard. "Stay right here," he called to Ryan as the helicopter rose in the air, "so the pilot can find you."

Ryan wanted to do exactly as his father said. He didn't want to wander off in the dark, scary forest. But Ling and Chu were determined to find the poachers. And Ryan didn't want to be left alone.

Chu tracked the poachers through the darkening forest, and Ling and Ryan followed breathlessly behind. At last they came to a cave. Smoke curled out of the opening. Someone was inside.

"The poachers!" whispered Ling.

Just then Ryan heard the helicopter circling overhead. He ran out to wave, to shout, "Here we are! Here we are!" But Chu pulled him back.

"The poachers will see us!" Ling hissed, annoyed at the silly American boy.

Ryan sighed as the helicopter flew away. He looked at the stars coming out in the night sky. Soon it would be too dark for the pilot to see anything.

Looks like I'm stuck here for the night, Ryan thought. And even worse, he was stuck with a girl who didn't like him one bit.

The next morning the sun rose clear and bright. "Breakfast," said Ling, handing Ryan a piece of dried meat.

"Breakfast?" said Ryan. "This is a doggie treat."

Ling gave him a look, and Ryan ate hurriedly. After all, he *was* hungry —and it was the perfect time to rescue the panda. The poachers had left the cave to hunt for food. Quickly, Ryan and Ling snuck inside.

Hearing the noise, the little panda poked his soft, furry head out of a basket. Ryan gazed at his big, sad eyes and had to smile. "So that's what all the fuss is about," he said, finally understanding.

"We have to go!" said Ling. "The panda needs his mother's milk!"

Ryan, Ling, and Chu hurried back toward the tractor. "Grandfather knows a shortcut," Ling explained as they came to a broken-down bridge.

Ryan stopped short, eyeing the rotted planks, the steep drop, and the rushing water below.

"It's safe," Chu called back, going on ahead.

Ryan hung back, afraid.

"Are you scared? Of a little bridge? Ha!" said Ling. She grasped the cub tightly. Walking unsteadily, Ryan followed along behind. Slowly and carefully, they began to make their way across. But suddenly, they heard shouts. The poachers had found them!

Ling glanced over her shoulder, then quickened her pace. Not looking where she was going, she stepped in between two planks. "Ahh!" she cried as she fell through the space. The panda flew from her arms, landing on Ryan's back.

"Ling!" said Ryan, grabbing her arm and holding her steady. Then he heard angry voices, closer than ever. The poachers were approaching fast.

Ling's legs swung dangerously over the roaring river. "Don't let go!" she pleaded. "I can't swim."

"I won't!" promised Ryan.

All at once, the other planks gave way. Ling, Ryan, and the panda all plunged down into the raging water below.

Ryan held on tight to Ling, just as he promised. Together, the three swirled around and around the wild and furious river. Finally, they came to rest on a muddy bank. Ling hugged the panda close, glad they'd all made it to safety. "Everyone is okay!" she told Ryan, checking her backpack for supplies. "But the meat sticks are gone."

Then Ling spotted the tracking collar. "Dr. Tyler can find us!" she shouted. Excited now, she tried to switch it on. But the battery was dead.

Ryan sighed. "What makes you think they're looking for us anyway?" he asked. "It wouldn't be the first time my dad forgot about me."

Ling looked at him, surprised. "Your father is proud of you. He reads your letters to everyone! He never forgets you."

Ryan wasn't sure. But Ling was right. At that very moment, Michael—recovered from his injury—was searching desperately for his son. All day long he'd been combing the forest—first by air and then by foot. "Where could they have gone?" he wondered frantically. "Where are Ryan, Ling, and Chu?"

At last, as the sun set slowly, Michael found Chu near the tractor. "The children fell from a great height," Chu told him. "I do not think they survived. Ling had the tracking collar. Remember? She would signal, if she could." A tear rolled down the old man's cheek.

"We've got to keep looking!" said Michael, not giving up. He'd brought Ryan to China to spend time with him, to show him he cared. And this is what happened? He had to find him! "As soon as the sun comes up, I'll be back here, searching."

That night Ryan and Ling huddled in a hollowed-out tree. The hungry panda cub, nestled between them, barked sorrowfully. Then he nuzzled Ryan's chin. Ling smiled. "I think he likes you," she said. Ryan hugged the panda close, falling fast asleep.

The next morning, Ling woke Ryan up early. Then she led him to a trail of moss-covered rocks. Carefully, they made their way over the slippery stones—until suddenly, they lost their footing!

Slipping and sliding, the three tumbled about. "Oh no!" cried Ryan.
They had landed at the top of a giant waterfall.

Whoosh! They shot down the rapids into a pool of slimy moss.
The muck covered them from head to foot. Without a second
thought, they jumped into the clear water of the river.

Suddenly, Ryan heard a noise. *Beep, beep, beep!* It was coming from his wristwatch. The alarm went off, reminding Ryan it was time to watch his favorite TV show. Ryan almost laughed. Watching TV with his friend Johnny? It all seemed so far away. Then Ryan realized something.

"My watch!" he cried. "It has a battery! We can put it in the collar!" Ryan jumped out of the water and raced to the shore. Ling followed his lead, and a moment later, they had the tracking collar working.

Beep, beep, beep! At the compound, Michael rushed to the tracking board and saw the blinking red light. A look of hope crossed his face. "Ryan!"

But Ling and Ryan couldn't wait for Michael to find them. Time was running out for the little panda and they had to get to the reserve. Once again, they trudged through the forest.

How much further do we have to go? Ryan wondered. They were all hungry, and the cub desperately needed his mother's milk. Maybe we're getting close, he thought, noticing the forest had changed to farmland.

All at once, the cub jumped from Ryan's arms and ran through a cornfield. "Catch him!" shouted Ling.

The cub raced up and down the rows of corn, with Ryan and Ling chasing behind. Suddenly, Ryan stopped short. A fierce-looking man dressed in long Tibetan robes blocked his way.

Ling stepped behind Ryan, whispering, "I don't understand much Tibetan. But I think he is mad."

Just then the cub poked his head out between the stalks. The Tibetan man smiled. "Come with me, protectors of our friend, the panda," he said.

The Tibetan elder led Ryan and Ling to his village. The two rested, then fed on delicious local dishes. But the poor little cub wouldn't take any food—not even yak milk from a bottle.

"We will sleep here tonight," said Ling. "Tomorrow we will get the panda cub back to the reserve."

Ryan gazed at the little cub—so playful, so sweet, so round. "He's sort of short and fat. Just like my friend Johnny."

"Jah-Ni?" Ling said. "That is Chinese. It means the best in the forest. I like it."

Ryan grinned. They had named the panda. Together.

Early the next morning, Ryan and Ling were awoken by loud voices. "The poachers!" Ling cried. "They cannot find Jah-Ni!"

Ryan thought quickly. "In here!" he said, waving at potato sacks lined up against the wall. "We'll hide in the sacks!"

A few minutes later, villagers loaded the sacks onto a cart. Ryan held his breath as the horse trotted slowly away. Maybe his plan would work! But the squirming panda cub tried to climb out of his sack. The poachers pointed and shouted. Sensing danger, the horse broke into a wild gallop.

Racing through the forest, the horse dragged the bouncing, bumping cart behind him. Finally the cart broke loose. Helter-skelter it rolled out of control, careening downhill. *Bang!* It crashed into a tree.

One by one, Ryan, Ling, and Jah-Ni crawled out from the overturned cart. Everyone was okay. But now, a huge mountain range towered above them. "The reserve is on the other side," said Ling. "The mountains are too dangerous to climb. Very steep. A lot of fog. It would take a day to go around."

Ryan patted the sickly cub. "We don't have a day."

Ryan and Ling began to climb. The going was rough, and both were exhausted when they came to a ledge—a ledge that came to a dead end.

"We must turn around," said Ling. But they couldn't do that either—the poachers were blocking their way!

The two men moved in...coming closer...and closer still. There was nowhere to run; nowhere to go. Ryan and Ling tried to fight them off. But they couldn't hold out. The men grabbed Jah-Ni!

"Ryan! Ling!" called a voice. It was Michael! He had tracked them down! Quickly, he swung onto the ledge, knocking the two men out. Jah-Ni flew high into the air. *Crash!* He landed on a tree branch just below the ledge.

"I've got to save him!" cried Ryan, jumping down, too.

"Ryan! That branch can't hold you!" Michael warned. But Ryan didn't listen. He crawled out on the limb. The panda cub held out his little arms, and Ryan pulled him close.

CRACK! The branch snapped!

Michael flung himself on the ground and, in a flash, scooped Ryan and the cub up to safety.

"You could have been killed!" Michael whispered, hugging Ryan tight.

"I'm okay, Dad," Ryan said. "But Jah-Ni's real sick. We have to hurry."

Quickly, they tied the poachers to the back of the trailer. Then they raced through the forest and back to the reserve. There, the mother panda reached out, drawing her baby close. The cub was going to be fine! The reserve would stay open!

Ling came up behind Ryan and kissed him quickly on the cheek. "I had a fun time," she said. "You are not spoiled after all. You are very brave."

Ryan blushed happily. Then Michael walked over and hugged Ryan close. "We need somebody to look after these pandas for the summer. Want a job?"

Ryan's smile grew wide. He understood now that his dad really loved him—and he understood, too, how important his dad's work really was. Ryan's gaze fell on the mother and baby panda, cuddling and nuzzling each other. It was going to be a terrific summer—for everybody!